Rib
Ticklers

Alan Gibbons

First published in Great Britain in 2010
by Caboodle Books Ltd
Copyright © Alan Gibbons 2010

A Catalogue record for this book is available
from the British Library.

ISBN 978 0 9565 239 69

Cover and Illustrations by Mark Stanley
Page Layout by Highlight Type Bureau Ltd
Printed by Cox and Wyman

The paper and board used in the paperback by
Caboodle Books Ltd are natural recyclable products
made from wood grown in sustainable forests.
The manufacturing processes conform to the environmental
regulations of the country of origin.

Caboodle Books Ltd
Riversdale, 8 Rivock Avenue, Steeton, BD20 6SA
www.authorsabroad.com

Contents

Gordon and the Beanstalk

Who wouldn't want Gordon Bigenuff as a neighbour? He was gentle and kind. He never played his music too loud. He would give anyone a helping hand. He was just the sweetest, loveliest man you could meet. He lived quietly at number ten, Stalktop Lane, Cloudly with a hen, a singing harp and – so some said – rather a lot of money.

There is one thing you should know about Gordon Bigenuff. As his name suggests he was, well, rather a large man. Let's not beat about the bush.

He was enormous.

He was massive.

He was colossal.

He was .... a giant.

But he lived on top of a cloud so nobody bothered him. He led a carefree life. Every day he tended his vegetable patch. He grew marrows and cabbages, carrots and turnips, but definitely no beans. Beans had caused his poor father Gary an awful lot of trouble in the old days when giant-killers roamed the Earth. A wicked scoundrel called Jack had stolen from Gary. It had been the death of Gordon's dear old Dad.

Gordon wiped away a tear as he thought about his poor father's terrible end. He wandered over to the edge of his cloud world and looked down. He trembled as he gazed at the world below.

He prayed that nobody would find the kind of magic beans that made giant beanstalks grow. Who knows what kind of wicked hooligan might climb up?

*   *   *

Little did Gordon know that, at that very moment, a pesky bundle of naughtiness by the name of John Jonesey Jones was selling his poor old mum's best cow for – guess what – a bag of brightly coloured magic beans!

"Be careful where you plant them, son," the proud new owner of the Jones family's cow said. "I dropped one down a grid once and it tore up the whole road."

Jonesey heard the story and his eyes twinkled with mischief. As he walked home he thought about all the places he could plant his beans.

One could go under nosey Mrs Parker's house.

No more twitching curtains.

One could go under the kennel of the dog next door.

No more barking.

One could go under his school.

No more Maths.

By the time Jonesey got home he was chuckling with delight at the thought of all the things he could do with his magic beans.

Then he saw his mum.

He swallowed. Hard.

His heart beat. Fast.

His skin went. Goosebumpy.

You see, his mum was waiting at the garden gate. Mrs Joan Jonesey Jones had the worst temper of any mother in the whole wide world.

Ever.

"I see you sold the cow," she said, crossing her arms.

"I did," said Jonesey, quaking in his boots.

"I hope you got a good price," she said, looking down her nose at him.

Jonesey said nothing.

"Jonesey?" Mum said, frowning.

"Yes, Mum?" said Jonesey, biting his lip.

"Show me what you got for the cow," Mum said.

"I'd rather not," said Jonesey, trembling.

"It isn't ...... beans, is it?" Mum asked.

"It might be," Jonesey said.

"Is it?" Mum asked.

"Yes," Jonesey croaked.

Mum gave him a clip round the ear.

Then a smack on the bottom.

Seconds later Mrs Jones was chasing Jonesey round and round the garden with a rolled up newspaper in her hand.

"You good-for-nothing nitwit!" she yelled.

She took the beans and threw them out of the window then she whacked him on the legs with the newspaper.

That night Jonesey went to bed without any supper. He fell asleep wishing he had never bought those stupid beans

But in the night the beans grew....and grew.....and grew.

Next morning Jonesey woke up and saw the biggest beanstalk he had seen in his whole life. So he started to climb.

*　　　　*　　　　*

Gordon woke bright and early and kicked off the bedclothes. He padded across his bedroom floor in his pyjamas and stockinged feet and counted his gold coins. He smiled happily. At last he had saved enough money to go on holiday to Red Rose Island. He was going to take his sweetheart Gertie Skyscraper away with him and ask her to marry him. He had been waiting for this moment for such a long time.

He patted the sack of gold coins happily and went to cook his breakfast.

He was tucking into his second sausage, which was as big as a boat, when he heard something.

He looked over his right shoulder.

Nobody there.

He looked over his left shoulder.

Nobody there.

He shrugged his shoulders and tucked into a rasher of bacon, which was as big as a carpet, when he heard the noise again.

He looked over his right shoulder.

Nobody there.

He looked over his left shoulder.

Nobody there.

Then he looked over his right shoulder again.

And there was Jonesey reaching for the sack of money with his thieving hands.

"No!" cried Gordon.

Jonesey snatched the bag and set off across the vegetable patch towards the beanstalk. Gordon gave chase, but, by the time he reached the end of the vegetable patch Jack was halfway down the beanstalk.

The money was gone. Gordon's tears fell like rain.

There would be no holiday to Red Rose Island.

There would be no marriage to lovely Gertie Skyscraper.

Gordon consoled himself by patting Henrietta who laid his golden eggs. Maybe she could lay enough of those special eggs to pay for the holiday then things would be all right.

*   *   *

But Jonesey wasn't done yet.

Next morning he climbed up the beanstalk again.

This time Gordon was in the bath when he heard something.

He put down his rubber duck and listened.

Nobody there.

He washed the shampoo out of his eyes and listened again.

Nobody there.

Then he heard the noise. He listened very hard and there they were, Jonesey's footsteps.

Gordon leapt from the bath and wrapped the towel round himself.

Jonesey was reaching for Henrietta the hen and her golden eggs.

"No!" Gordon cried

Jonesey snatched Henrietta and set off across the vegetable patch towards the beanstalk. Gordon gave chase, but, by the time he reached the end of the vegetable patch Jack was halfway down the beanstalk.

Henrietta and the eggs were gone. Once more Gordon's tears fell like rain.

There would be no holiday to Red Rose Island.

There would be no marriage to Gertie Skyscraper.

Gordon consoled himself by listening to his singing harp Harriet. Maybe people would pay enough money to listen to her beautiful singing voice to pay for the holiday then things would be all right.

*   *   *

Jonesey still wasn't satisfied.

His mum didn't just have the worst temper of any mother in the whole wide world.

She was also the greediest mother in the whole wide world.

Ever.

She gave Jonesey a great, big smile when he brought the sack of gold coins home.

But when he brought home Henrietta, the hen that laid the golden eggs, she hugged him so hard he almost broke in two.

Jonesey liked making her happy. It was better to be a hero than a nitwit. So up that beanstalk he climbed one last time.

This time Gordon was ready for Jonesey. He lay awake waiting. It wasn't long before he smelled Jonesey's sweaty socks.

Gordon got out of bed.

Jonesey was reaching for Harriet the singing harp.

Harriet cried: "Help!"

Gordon cried: "Stop!"

Jonesey snatched Harriet and set off across the vegetable patch towards the beanstalk. Gordon gave chase. This time Jack had only just started his climb back to the ground. Gordon made a grab for Jack. Jack ducked and scrambled down the beanstalk. Gordon followed.

Jack had just reached the bottom when he heard a loud cry of panic. Gordon had slipped. Jonesey looked up just in time to see the giant's enormous bottom hurtling towards him. Jonesey froze. He was so scared he couldn't move an inch.

Gordon's colossal shadow spread around Jonesey.

Gordon's huge bottom loomed above Jonesey.

Then – thump – Gordon landed smack on top of Jonesey and squashed the poor boy as flat as a pancake.

Jonesey's mum had heard the noise. She ran out of the house.

"Where's my little John Jonesey Jones?" she cried.

Gordon picked himself up.

"Oops!" he said.

Jonesey's mum stared at her little boy. Her eyes were round with horror.

"You've flattened him," she cried. "My poor little boy. I love him so."

This time it was mum's turn to shed tears like rain.

"I'll give everything back," she told Gordon. "You can take your money. You can take your hen. You can take your harp. Just help my lovely little boy."

Gordon thought for a moment, then he thought some more, then he had an idea.

"Have you got a bike pump?" he asked.

"There's one in the shed," said Mrs Jonesey Jones.

Gordon rummaged in the shed for a few moments then he returned with the bike pump. He popped the valve in Jonesey's belly button.

Then he pumped....

and pumped....

and pumped.

Jonesey started to fill with air.

He swelled...

and swelled....

and swelled.

Soon he was as round as a ball.

"You've put too much air in him," cried Mrs Jonesey Jones. "He's going to burst!"

So Gordon let out some air, just enough to return Jonesey to his normal self.

Mrs Jonesey Jones thanked Gordon and gave him back his sack of gold coins, Henrietta the hen and Harriet the harp.

John Jonesey Jones thanked Gordon and promised to be good.

So Gordon climbed back up the beanstalk.

Next morning he called on Gertie Skyscraper and they started to plan their holiday. A week later on a pure white beach, under a golden sun, in front of swaying palm trees Gordon asked Gertie to marry him.

And Gertie said yes.

And they all lived…well, you know that bit, don't you?

Batman,

A lean machine

In his crime busting youth,

Eats so much junk food they call him...

Fatman.

You're not a woodcutter, you're a very naughty boy!

Once upon a time, not so long ago, there was a beautiful princess called Snow White. Her hair was as glossy and black as a raven's wing. Her skin was as fair and white as the flesh of a ripe banana. Her lips were as red as the setting sun. All in all, she was….absolutely beautiful!

Now everybody loved Snow White. The little birds in the trees swooned and tumbled from their perches when she passed. The little bunny rabbits froze in mid-hop and stared entranced at her loveliness. The medium-sized deer were so taken with her that they walked into walls and lay stunned on the ground. The big brown bears fell under her spell too and blundered about in a daze.

Every day Snow White dreamed that a handsome prince would arrive at the palace gates and ask for her hand- and the rest of her- in marriage. She wandered the grounds singing her favourite song.

"Someday my prince will come."

Her voice was as sweet as a sticky bun.

Not everybody loved Snow White. Her wicked stepmother Queen Beryl was so jealous of the pretty princess her nose would occasionally turn into a Brussels sprout. She stomped up and down in a hissy fit and kicked any sleeping cat in her path. Her grumpiness knew no bounds. She knew the palace disco was just a few days away and she was desperate to be the prettiest woman there, the Belle of the Ball.

She marched into the bathroom and spoke to her magic mirror Kevin.

"Mirror, mirror above the loo,

who's the loveliest?

Who? Who? Who?"

But Kevin, who was a very honest mirror, said:

"Not you, chuck, compared to Snow White you look like the back of a bus."

(That was a horse-drawn omnibus, of course. Motor buses hadn't been invented yet.)

Queen Beryl was furious. Her eyes blazed. Her chin wobbled. Smoke came out of her nostrils. She stamped into her bedroom and looked at her brand new pink tracksuit, the one she was going to wear to the palace disco. She decided it was time to get rid of that pesky Snow White.

Next morning she called Billy the Woodcutter in for a chat.

"Billy," she said, "here's a crisp, new ten pound note. Pop down to the DIY store and buy the sharpest axe they've got."

Billy was puzzled. "But I've got an axe already," he said.

Queen Beryl smiled her wickedest smile. "This one has got to be especially sharp," she said. "I want you to chop off Snow White's head."

Billy was shocked. "I can't do that," he said. "It's not legal."

"Billy," Queen Beryl said. "Either you chop off Snow White's head or I will order my guards to chop yours off."

Reluctantly Billy agreed to do the dirty deed. He popped down to the DIY store and bought the sharpest axe they had. Then he went looking for Snow White. He found her making daisy chains.

"Come on, Snowy girl," he said. "Let's go for a picnic."

They packed some meat pies and some jam donuts and set off towards Bluebell Wood. They laid a crisp, white tablecloth on the grass and started their picnic.

Snow White was tucking into her meat pie when Billy sneaked behind her and pulled out the brand new axe. He was about to swing it at Snow White's elegant neck when a little bird sang out a warning.

"Look out, look out, Snow White," the bird tweeted. "He's got an axe."

Billy swiftly hid the axe behind his back. Snow White turned and stared at him.

"Is it true?" she asked. "Have you got an axe?"

"Of course not," Billy said. "Why would I bring my axe on a picnic?"

"Liar, liar, pants on fire," protested the little bird.

His name was Bert. Bert the bird.

Snow White looked at Billy for a moment then she turned round and finished off her pie. She was a very trusting young lady. The moment she started to tuck into her jam donut Billy pulled out the axe again. Instantly, a little bunny rabbit shouted a warning.

"It's true," she cried, "he *does* have an axe and he *was* going to chop off your pretty head."

Once more Billy hid the axe.

"Is it true?" Snow White asked. "Have you got an axe, Billy?"

"I told you," Billy said. "I don't have an axe."

The little bunny rabbit had had enough. She had been working out at the local gym and she had muscles the size of footballs. She hopped up to Billy and snatched the axe out of his hand.

Her name was Dagnabbit.

Dagnabbit the rabbit.

"What do you call this?" she demanded. "Scotch mist?"

Billy hung his head. "Oops," he said.

"Oops?" said Snow White. "Oops! Is that all you've got to say?"

"I'm very sorry," said Billy, shifting his feet unhappily.

"Honestly," Snow White said. "You're not a woodcutter, you're a very naughty boy."

She had seen way too many movies.

"Did Queen Beryl put you up to this?" she asked.

Billy nodded.

Snow White thought for a moment then she came up with a brilliant plan.

"Listen Billy," she said. "You can make up for your wickedness. Would you like that?"

"Oh, yes please," said Billy. He knew he had been a silly Billy.

Snow White picked up a bottle of tomato ketchup and splashed it on the axe head.

"Take this to Queen Beryl," Snow White said. "She will think the ketchup is my blood. It will give me time to find somewhere to hide from Her Wickedness."

So Billy took the axe to Queen Beryl. Sure enough the wicked queen thought the ketchup was blood. She sang a happy, little song:

"She's dead, she's dead,

that horrible girl is dead.

She's dead. She's dead. She's dead.

She's .... DEAD!""

Now she really would be the prettiest woman at the disco, the Belle of the Ball.

Meanwhile Snow White was picking her way through the forest. It was getting dark and she was scared. Shadows crept. Night winds blew. Wild creatures stirred. Suddenly she spotted a beautiful little cottage in a clearing. She tiptoed towards it.

"Is anybody home?" she asked.

Nobody was. Luckily for Snow White the door was open. She crept inside and looked around. Everything was tiny. The tables were tiny. The chairs were tiny. Even the beds were tiny. The house owners must be tiny too. Each of the seven beds had a little plaque attached with the name of the owner on it. Snow White read the names:

Incy.

Wincy.

Hunky.

Chunky.

Stinky.

Blinky.

And last of all….Bob.

Snow White was very tired and stressed so she lay down on Bob's bed and fell fast asleep.

At that very moment, at the Sticky Toffee mines in the Marshmallow Mountains the owners of the house, seven dwarfs who were known to everyone as…the Seven Dwarfs, had just finished work.

"Hi ho," they sung. "Hi ho, hi ho,

It's home from work we go,

With a bag of chips and some juicy, red lips,

Hi ho, hi ho, hi ho."

Their lanterns bobbed through the thickening darkness. When they arrived home they saw Snow White curled up on Bob's bed, fast asleep.

"Oh lads, you shouldn't have," he said. "How did you know it was my birthday? Who bought me this girl out of the mail order catalogue?"

The dwarfs shook their heads.

"We didn't order her," Hunky said, "and it isn't your birthday, you peabrain. She's a trespasser. She might even be…a burglar."

So Bob woke Snow White.

"Are you a trespasser?" he asked, a little bit frightened. "Or even a burglar?"

"I am neither," said Snow White. "I am a runaway princess. Wicked Queen Beryl tried to kill me."

"Kill you!" gasped the Seven Dwarfs.

"That's right," said Snow White, "she told a woodcutter to chop off my head."

"Oh, you need your head," Chunky said. "It's hard to think without it. And where would you put your hat?"

"She tried to kill me to death," Snow White said, "and that is by far the worst way. May I stay here? I have nowhere to go."

So the Seven Dwarfs cleared out the room above the garage where they kept their motorbikes. (They had just been invented by a very smart elf called Monty the Mechanic). For a while Snow White was safe.

But that night wicked Queen Beryl marched into her bathroom and spoke to her magic mirror Kevin.

"Mirror, mirror above the loo,
who's the loveliest?
Who? Who? Who?"

To her horror Kevin gave her the same answer as the day before.

"Not you, chuck, compared to Snow White you're like the back of a bus."

(This was a motor bus. Monty the Mechanic had just invented that too.)

Wicked queen Beryl flew into a towering rage.

21

"That Billy," she cried, "he's not a woodcutter, he's a very naughty boy."

She had been watching the same movies as Snow White.

Queen Beryl decided to deal with Snow White herself.

"I'll do this myself," she said.

She mixed a magic potion. It bubbled and steamed. She drank it down. Instantly there was an amazing transformation. Within moments she had turned into a shrivelled, warty old lady.

"She will never recognize me," said wicked Queen Beryl.

By the time she found the Seven Dwarfs' cottage, the dwarfs were back at work and Snow White was alone in the house. Queen Beryl rang the doorbell.

(This was another of Monty the Mechanic's inventions).

Snow White answered the door and said: "Hello, shrivelled, warty old lady. What do you want?"

Queen Beryl held out her hand. "Good morning, my dear. There is a special offer at our supermarket. Would you like to try our new chocolate bar?"

Snow White said she would. She took one bite of the poisoned chocolate bar and crumpled to the floor, apparently dead as a doorknob. Wicked Queen Beryl skipped away down the road, cackling.

"Now I will be the Belle of the Ball," she said.

An hour later the Seven Dwarfs arrived home, singing their song:

"Hi ho, hi ho, it's home from work we go,

with a bag of chips and some juicy red lips.

Hi ho, hi ho, hi ho."

When they worked through the door the Seven Dwarfs saw Snow White lying on the floor, apparently dead.

"Just look at that!" said Stinky. "We only got this girl yesterday and she's broken already."

"Maybe she needs new batteries," said Blinky.

But there was nowhere for the batteries to go.

"I'll put her out for the binmen," said Incy.

"You can't put her out for the binmen," said Wincy, horrified.

"Put her down," said Bob. "Let me see."

Fortunately, Bob was a medical student in his spare time. He took Snow White's pulse.

"She's not dead," he said. "She's in a coma." He went to get his medical book. "Here we are. Somebody has fed her a poisoned chocolate bar. She will be in a deep sleep for a thousand years."

"That's terrible," Stinky said. "Isn't there anything we can do?"

"Let's see," Bob said, leafing through the book. "Yes, here it is. There is an antidote. If we can find the most handsome prince in the whole world he can make her better."

"How?" Blinky asked.

"There's only one way to wake her up," said Bob. "He has to give her a big, sloppy kiss on her ruby red lips."

The other dwarfs giggled. They were very immature.

A few moments later they were starting up their motorbikes. (This was another of Monty the Mechanic's inventions, remember).

They roared off down the M1. After about an hour they spotted a glittering castle.

They left the motorway and made their way to the castle door. They knocked as hard as they could. Soon a very handsome prince appeared.

"Wow," Bob said, "you've got to be the most handsome prince in the universe."

"That's true," the prince said.

He was a very nice prince but he certainly wasn't modest.

"What's your name?" asked Stinky.

"I am Prince Hunky O'Gorgeous," said the prince.

The dwarfs thought it was an amazing coincidence. He was gorgeous by name and gorgeous by nature. They showed him a photo of Snow White.

(The camera was Monty the Mechanic's first invention).

Prince Hunky thought she was very beautiful and agreed to give her a big, sloppy kiss better. The Dwarfs rode back to their little cottage in the woods. Prince Hunky rode pillion. He swept Snow White up in his muscular arms and gave her a great big kiss. Her eyes fluttered open.

"It's working," said Bob. "Kiss her again."

Prince Hunky gave Snow White another sloppy kiss.

She looked at him and said, "At last, my prince has come."

It was love at first sight so they got married that very afternoon. They went to the palace to tell wicked Queen Beryl what they thought of her. The disco was in full swing. Queen Beryl was in the middle of the dance floor in her brand new pink tracksuit. She was doing the conga. Suddenly there was a loud bang and a puff of smoke and she vanished. Nobody had mentioned that her magic potion caused complications. A little beetle ran away into the woods and was never seen again. Nor was Queen Beryl. Guess what. Snow White, Prince Hunky and the Seven Dwarfs all lived happily ever after.

As for Monty the Mechanic, he invented a money-making machine and lived very wealthily ever after.

Robin Hood
Was extremely good.
Those arrows of his he shot 'em
Where?
Why straight at the sheriff's bottom!

The Three Quite Big Pigs

Three little pigs and their mum (that makes four pigs) lived in a house somewhere in England. The house was very cramped and cluttered. To be honest, it was a bit of a pigsty.

One morning Percy Pig woke up with his brother Peter's trotter sticking in his ribs. He was very uncomfortable. At the same moment Polly Pig woke up with Percy's curly whirly tail sticking up her left nostril. She was very uncomfortable too. The three little pigs started fighting. Soon they were having a right old punch up.

Mum heard the noise and stormed into the room. "What is all this noise about?" she cried. "Stop that fighting right now!"

The three little pigs stopped.

"Get out of bed," said Mummy Pig. "I want to see what the problem is."

She realized what was wrong immediately. "I can see the problem," she said. "You're not little piglets any more. You're great big porkers."

The three little pigs looked at each other. It was true. They were really three quite big pigs.

"I am going to pack you a sandwich each," Mum said. "I am going to give you a biscuit and a bottle of pop. It is high time you went out into the big, wide world and got yourself a job and somewhere to live."

"Yes Mum," said Polly Pig.

"Yes Mum," said Peter Pig.

"Do I have to?" said Percy Pig who was a bit of a mummy's boy.

"Yes, you do," said Mum. "You can't hang onto my apron strings forever."

So the three quite big pigs set off to find a job and a house. They were about to turn the corner at the top of the street when Mum shouted after them. "Oh, I forgot to tell you," Mum said. "Look out for the big, bad Hum Ha Whooo."

"What's the big, bad Hum Ha Whooo?" asked Percy Pig.

"She means the wolf," said Polly. "Don't you know anything? He eats little pigs, probably quite big ones too."

Percy started to tremble. He really was a mummy's boy.

The three quite big pigs hadn't gone very far when they heard a strange noise. It worried them….a lot.

"Hum Bubba Ha, Hum Bubba Ha,

I smell sausage. I smell bacon.

I smell….piggywig."

Immediately Percy Pig started to tremble again. He was a mummy's boy and a bit of a cowardly custard. He looked around and his eyes lit on a bale of straw.

"I'm not going one step further," he said. "I'm going to build myself a straw house."

"Oh, don't be a dopey dimbo," said Peter and Polly. "The big bad wolf will soon blow a straw house down.

But Percy wouldn't listen. He was staying put.

"Fair enough," said Peter and Polly. "If you run into trouble come and find us."

Then off they went down the road.

Percy had just finished building his straw house when he heard the wolf coming.

"Hum Bubba Ha, Hum Bubba Ha,

I smell sausage, I smell bacon,

I smell piggywig.."

Percy sat inside his straw houses with his knickety knockety knees knocking.

He heard the wolf prowling round his house.

"Hum Bubba Ha, Hum Bubba Ha.,

Hum Bubba Ha, Ha, Ha.

I smell sausage. I smell bacon.

I smell piggywig.

I'm a-going to huff, I'm a-going to puff.

I'm a-going to blow your house right down."

"Oh, not by the hair on my chinny chin chin," said Percy.

But the wolf huffed, and he puffed and he blew the house down.

Moments later Percy Pig was fleeing with his curly whirly tail going ding-a-ling-a-ling all the way down the lane.

At that moment Peter Pig was getting tired.

"Give me a carry," he said.

"Don't be silly," said Polly Pig. "You're bigger than I am. I can't carry you, you big pudding."

Peter Pig looked round and his eyes lit on a pile of sticks.

"I'm not going one step further," he said. "I'm going to build myself a stick house."

"Oh, don't be a muddled muppet," said Polly. "The big bad wolf will soon blow a stick house down."

But Peter wouldn't listen. He was staying put.

"Fair enough," said Polly. "If you run into trouble come and find me."

She set off down the road.

Peter had just finished building his stick house when he heard his brother coming.

"Help help," Percy cried. "The big bad wolf, the big bad wolf, help, help, the big, bad wolf,

he's after me."

Peter let Percy in. They sat inside the stick house with their knickety knackety knees knocking together. They heard the wolf prowling round the house.

"Hum Bubba Ha, Hum Bubba Ha,

Hum Bubba, Ha, Ha, Ha,

I smell sausage, I smell bacon,

I smell piggywig.

I'm a-going to huff, I'm a-going to puff,

I'm a going to blow your house right down."

"Oh, not by the hair on our chinny chin chins," said Percy and Peter.

But the wolf huffed and he puffed and he blew the house down.

Now Percy and Peter Pig were fleeing with their curly whirly tails going ding-a-ling-a-ling all down the lane.

By this time Polly Pig had been to the builder's yard. She had ordered some bricks and cement, some tiles and some double-glazed windows. She had ordered some furniture and cable TV. She had a red hot curry bubbling away over the fire and she had just settled down to watch Manchester United against Liverpool on the TV. She was making herself a nice pot of tea when she heard her brothers rushing down the road.

"Help, help,

the big bad wolf, the big bad wolf,

the big bad wolf is after....US!" they cried.

Polly let them in the house and put the bolts on. The three quite big pigs sat on the sofa and waited for the wolf to arrive.

"Here he comes," said Percy.

He was trembling like a leaf. What a mummy's boy.

The wolf arrived.

"Hum Bubba Ha, Hum Bubba Ha,

Hum Bubba Ha Ha Ha.

I'm a-going to huff, I'm a-going to puff,

I'm a-going to blow your house right down."

"Not by the hair on our chinny, chin chins," the three pigs shouted.

The wolf huffed and he puffed and...

Nothing.

The house was strongly built. Nothing happened.

The wolf looked this way. He looked that way. He couldn't understand it at all. That's when he spotted a door on the roof. There's the way in, he thought. It was the chimney, of course. He was a very silly wolf. Up the walls he climbed. Over the roof he crawled. He looked into the chimney and the smoke stung his eyes. He started to climb down the chimney.

Wiggle, wiggle, wiggle went his big fat bottom.

Wriggle, wriggle, wriggle went his big, furry tail.

But he hadn't reckoned with the red-hot curry.

"Something's burning," he said.

"Something's boiling," he said.

"Something's singeing," he said.

He looked down and saw the tip of his tail dangling in the red-hot curry.

"Oh crumbs," he said. "It's me! Yaroo!"

A moment later he was rocketing across the sky with his tail on fire. He landed with a great big splash in the farmer's pond, blowing on his tail to put out the flames. He sat there thinking.

Soon he came to a decision.

"That's the last time I go chasing after little pigs," he said. "From now on I am going to be the world's first vegetarian wolf. I am going to eat turnips on toast.

I am going to eat lettuce lasagne. I am going to eat chicory chocolate. I am going to eat sprout sandwiches. I am going to eat carrot custard. But not all together, of course."

Do you know what? He kept his word and he never chased another pig.

As for the three quite big pigs, they settled in to enjoy their new house. Percy became an ice cream salesman. Peter opened a flower shop. Polly went to university and became a lawyer.

Polly phoned Mum and she came round for tea.

They had one of Polly's red-hot curries. Percy made poppadoms and chutney. Peter made vegetable samosas.

They finished off the meal with some of the wolf's chicory chocolate.

Guess what? It was lovely!

Ann Boleyn grew rather thin
Trying to save her pure white skin.
She would have preferred to say in bed
The day she went and lost her head.

The Wimpy Gorilla and the Mighty Chimpanzee

In the jungle, halfway up a mountain, amid the rolling mist there lived a gorilla.

He was a huge gorilla. He was a grumpy gorilla. He had enormous muscles. His name was Gideon.

He woke one morning and scratched his belly. He stretched and yawned. Then he saw Charlie Chimp walking past. He peeled a banana and shoved it in Charlie's face. He laughed so hard he almost burst a blood vessel. He rolled on his back and kicked his legs in the air. He thought he was so funny, wiping off the banana gunk with a hankie.

Charlie didn't think it was funny at all. "That's mean," he said.

Gideon picked himself up. He stopped laughing. He frowned. He only laughed when he was making somebody else miserable. He really was a grumpy gorilla. He towered over Charlie and beat his chest.

"Do you want to make something of it, Mr Wimpy Chimpy?"

Charlie stared up at his monstrous neighbour. He swallowed hard.

"No," he said.

Next morning Gideon woke up and scratched his belly. Again. He stretched and yawned. Again. He saw Charlie walking past. Again. This time he picked up a big, hairy coconut and threw it.

Bonk! It hit Charlie on the head. Gideon laughed so hard he nearly wet himself. He rolled on his back and kicked his legs in the air. He thought it was hilarious.

Charlie didn't. "That's cruel," he said.

Gideon picked himself up. He stopped laughing. He frowned. He was the grumpiest gorilla on the mountain. He towered over Charlie and beat his chest.

"Do you want to make something of it?" he asked.

Charlie stared up at his mountainous neighbour. He gulped. "No," he said.

That night Charlie sat on a rock. He thought and thought. Then he thought some more. As the sun sank over the horizon he had an idea. He spent the next hour knotting creepers together.

"Right, Mr Gideon Gorilla," he told the moon, "I'm going to get even with you. You wait and see."

Next morning Gideon woke up and scratched his belly. As usual. He stretched and yawned. As usual. He saw Charlie watching him from some distance.

"What's up with you?" Gideon grumbled.

He was quite horribly grumpy that morning.

Charlie spoke up. "I bet I can beat you at tug of war," he said.

"Don't be silly," said Gideon, beating his chest. "You're a wimp and I'm a fine figure of an ape. It's no contest."

"I can still beat you," said Charlie.

"Can't," said Gideon.

"Can too," Charlie insisted. "Let me show you."

He looked around, pretending to search for a suitable creeper.

He picked up one end of the one he had prepared earlier.

"Here," he said.

Gideon yawned and held the creeper between his finger and thumb.

"This will be as easy as eating bananas," he said.

Charlie picked up his end of the creeper. What Gideon couldn't see was that Charlie was holding it, not by the end, but in the middle. The creeper ran into the bushes. Charlie had tied the other end to the biggest, strongest tree in the jungle.

"I'm going to pull you past that rock," he said.

"No you're not," said Gideon.

"Yes," Charlie said, "I am."

Gideon gave a playful tug, expecting to see Charlie go tumbling over. Charlie let the creeper run through his hands.

"Easy," Gideon said.

Then the creeper pulled taut and stopped. Gideon pulled. Nothing happened.

"Wimp," Charlie said cheekily.

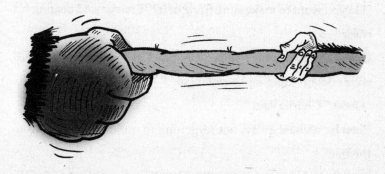

Gideon frowned and gripped the creeper in his fist. He pulled again. Nothing happened.

"Weakling," Charlie chuckled.

This time Gideon heaved with all his might. Once more nothing happened. Gideon tugged and tugged, yanked and pulled. He stared in disbelief at Charlie. This was one strong chimp. Soon Gideon was grunting with the effort. Still he couldn't pull Charlie.

"This is impossible," Gideon panted.

He hauled on the rope with all his might. Soon he was gasping for air. Charlie could see he was completely exhausted. He gave one sharp pull on the rope and Gideon fell flat on his face in the mud.

Beaten.

Defeated.

All the monkeys laughed at Gideon the wimpy gorilla. All the birds cackled at Gideon the loser. As Gideon lay there, Charlie towered over him.

"This is impossible," Gideon whimpered.

"Do you want to make something of it?" Charlie said beating his chest.

Gideon threw up his hands. "No. No. I've learned my lesson. I won't do anything mean ever again."

"Good," Charlie said.

Then he walked away, not forgetting to untie the creeper from the tree.

Sometimes brains are better than brawn.

Santa's To Do List

Feed the reindeer,
Tick.
Load the presents,
Tick.
Thank the elves,
Tick.
Grease the sleigh runners,
Tick.
Hang out the red suit,
Tick.
Polish the black boots,
Tick.
Stow the map and compass,
Tick.
Go to bed early,
Tick.
Set the alarm clock,
Tick tock
Tick tock
Tick tock.

The boy with the silly name

Some of us have to carry a heavy burden through life. That was the case with a flame-haired lad from County Cork. His parents had given him the name of Chucklejack O'Hardyhaha. Now, some people have weird ideas when it comes to naming their children. They think that giving their son a ridiculous name will toughen him up.

But Mr and Mrs O'Hardyhaha didn't do their little boy any favours at all. The moment the school bullies discovered that he was called Chucklejack they teased him and poked him, pinched him and punched him. The only thing they didn't do was call him names. If your name is Chucklejack O'Hardyhaha it is hard to call you anything worse.

Chucklejack had a wretched childhood. The bullies weren't the only ones who thought his name was funny. So did the girls. Though young Chucklejack wasn't a bad-looking lad, none of them would have anything to do with him. If your name was Mary Kelly or Anne Hegarty you wouldn't want to get yourself hitched to one of the O'Hardyhahas, would you?

At the age of sixteen Chucklejack left his home village and went away to sea. The other sailors fell about laughing when the captain called out his name. The ship's parrot tried very hard to say his name but it came out Chachacha which wasn't really much of an improvement on the original.

One day there was a terrible storm and the ship ran aground on a South Sea Island. Even here, thousands of miles from home the name Chucklejack O'Hardyhaha provoked gales of laughter.

Chucklejack roamed the oceans wide until one day he came to a decision. He would change his name and join the crew of a new ship. As he clambered into his hammock that night one of the other men asked his name.

"It's Tom Molloy," said Chucklejack.

There followed the sweetest sound he ever did hear. It was the sound of silence. For the first time in Chucklejack's life nobody made fun of him. Nobody teased him. The days passed, then the weeks, then the months and Chucklejack enjoyed life as plain, ordinary Tom Molloy.

One blazing hot day the ship weighed anchor in the harbour of San Flamingo. The sailors left the ship to look around. The captain read out one of the posters that were pasted on every wall in the town:

Wanted

A husband for the royal princess

Let it be known that the Royal Family of San Flamingo is inviting suitors to present themselves at the royal palace. The princess has reached a marriageable age and...

Suddenly the captain's chin wobbled. His lip quivered. His eyes filled with tears.

"What's the matter, captain?" asked Chucklejack.

"Oh, no wonder they can't find anybody to marry the poor girl," the captain said. "The poster is signed by His Royal Highness Sprocketvalve Bananabucket."

At that the entire crew fell about laughing, all except Chucklejack. An idea was forming in his head.

At noon the next day Chucklejack presented himself at the palace at noon. When the gates opened he was the only suitor present. He walked through sumptuous gardens and enormous echoing halls. Finally, he reached the throne room itself.

There sat the King, His Majesty Sprocketvalve Bananabucket the Third. There had been two Bananabuckets before him. The King looked down at the unshaven, poorly dressed sailor.

"Are you the only suitor?" the King asked, disappointed.

"I think so, Your Majesty," said Chucklejack.

The King sighed. "Three years I have been trying to find a husband for my only daughter. I fear she will never be married. Every time they hear her name they burst out laughing, then they walk away shaking their heads."

42

"I'm not laughing," said Chucklejack.

"No," the King said, "You're not. Why not?"

"It is because," Chucklejack said, "my name is Chucklejack O'Hardyhaha."

The King stared. "Is this some kind of joke?" he asked.

"It is no joke," Chucklejack said.

The King clapped his hands. "Summon the princess," he said. He leaned forward. "If you laugh at her name I will have you taken out and flogged."

Chucklejack told the King he would not laugh.

The Prime Minister entered the room. Beside him walked the loveliest creature Chucklejack had ever seen in his life. She had a mane of flaming red hair that tumbled over alabaster shoulders. It was love at first sight.

"This is my daughter," the King said, "Princess Warblehoney Bananabucket."

He watched fiercely for any sign of a chuckle or a guffaw. Chucklejack didn't so much as laugh. All he could do was stare at the beautiful princess.

A brief courtship followed. A month later Chucklejack O'Hardyhaha married his lovely bride Warblehoney Bananabucket and they lived happily ever after and had four children.

There was the eldest, a charming boy called Whippetjuggler.

There were the twins, a good-natured girl called Semolina and her brother Frogspawn.

Finally there was the baby.

They called him Tom.

Nightmare

So bad
I woke up crying.
So bad
I felt depressed all morning.
So bad
it left me with a sick feeling
that put me off my dinner.
So *bad!*
I wonder why
I can't remember it.

The Three Billy Goats Woof

Not so very long ago three goats lived in a park in Liverpool.

The first goat was called Big Billy Goat Gruff because he was big.

The second goat was called Middling Billy Goat Gruff because he was medium sized.

The third and last goat was called Little Billy Goat Gruff because he was, well, very small. But he didn't like the name Little so he was known as Tiddler.

The three goats were brothers.

One morning Big woke up and gasped in horror. "Oh no."

Middling woke up next and groaned in dismay. "Oh dear."

Tiddler was the last to wake up and he hopped around demanding to know what was wrong.

"Just look at the ground," said Big. "We've eaten every blade of grass in this park, all the neighbouring parks, in fact the whole city."

Middling and Tiddler wailed in unison. "No!"

"I'm going to die," sobbed Tiddler. "My ribs will stick out and I will be as skinny as a drink straw."

"Now, now," said Big. "You're not going to die."

"Aren't I?' blubbed Tiddler, drying his eyes with his hoof.

"Of course not," said Big. "I have a plan."

This was Big's plan. The three goats would catch the number 100 bus to the Runcorn Bridge where it crosses the River Mersey.

They would cross the great bridge over the great river and live the rest of their lives in Cheshire munching the emerald green grass.

The three goats queued at the bus stop. Presently the number 100 bus appeared and they climbed on.

"Hold on, lads," said the bus driver. "Only people and dogs are allowed on this bus. You're not people. Are you some kind of dog? Say woof."

The goats bleated back.

"Close enough," said the driver. "All aboard."

Soon the bus stopped by the Runcorn Bridge and the goats got off.

"It's big," Tiddler said.

"Of course it's big," Big said. "It has to stretch all the way over the river."

"If it didn't," Middling said. "Everybody who walked across would get wet."

Tiddler set off immediately but Big grabbed him by the scruff of the neck.

"Not so fast," he said. "There's a problem."

The three goats stared at the bridge. Sure enough there was a problem. Smack in the middle of the bridge sat the biggest, ugliest creature you ever did see. He had long, green hair. He had big, googly eyes. He had a fat, whiskery face and thick, grey lips like car tyres. He had teeth like gravestones and a tongue like a slug. He was a troll.

"What do we do?" Tiddler asked.

Big thought for a moment. "One of us has got to go first," he said. He glanced at Middling. "You go."

"Oh no, not me," said Middling. He glanced at Tiddler. "You go."

"Oh no, not me," said Tiddler. He glanced round and realised that there was nobody else there.

He gazed at his brothers with big, sad eyes.

"Don't do those big, sad eyes at me," said Big. "I invented that look. He might take pity on a very small goat. Off you go."

So Tiddler set off trip, trap, trip, trap along the Runcorn Bridge. He had just got halfway when the Troll stood up, planted his feet and growled.

"I'm a troll, fol-de-roll.

I'm a troll, fol-de-roll.

And I'm going to eat you

For my supper!"

"Please don't eat me," bleated Tiddler. "I'm no bigger than a chocolate bar. Eat my brother. He's so much bigger and tastier."

The Troll looked at the two remaining goats. "Fine," he said. "There is more meat on those two. Off you go." Then he sat down to take the weight off his feet.

So Tiddler scampered trip trap, trip trap along the Runcorn Bridge. He got to the other side and started to munch the green, green grass of Cheshire.

Next it was the turn of Middling. He set off trip trap, trip trap along the Runcorn Bridge. He had just got halfway when the Troll stood up, planted his feet and growled.

"I'm a troll, fol-de-roll.

I'm a troll, fol-de-roll.

And I'm going to eat you

For my supper!"

"Please don't eat me," bleated Middling. "I'm no bigger than a bag of fish and chips. Eat my brother. He's so much bigger and tastier."

The Troll looked at the remaining goat. "Fine," he said. "There is more meat on him. Off you go." Then he sat down to take the weight off his feet.

So Middling scampered trip trap, trip trap along the Runcorn Bridge to the other side where he joined his younger brother

Tiddler eating the green, green grass of Cheshire.

Now it was the turn of the final goat, Big. He set off trip trap, trip trap along the Runcorn Bridge. He had just reached halfway when the Troll stood up, planted his feet and growled.

"I'm a Troll fol-de-roll.

I'm a Troll fol-de-roll.

And I'm going to eat you

For my supper!"

Big's eyes narrowed. He stared. He glared.

"So you're going to eat me, are you?" he asked.

"Definitely," said the Troll.

Without another word Big butted the Troll over the railings and down, down, down until the Troll landed with an enormous splash in the River Mersey.

"It's not fair," he said. "Last week there was a dragon from Dragon Lane. I said stop and he burned my eyebrows off."

He wiped away a tear. He did like those big, bushy eyebrows.

"Then there were seven little fellows from Bootle. I said stop but they ran between my legs. I'm going to turn over a new leaf and get a new job."

The Troll bobbed up and down for a few moments, feeling very sorry for himself, then he came to a decision. He swam to the riverbank, shook the water from his hair, rang out his underpants and set off for the number 100 bus into Liverpool.

First he went to the barber's shop and got his hair styled.

Then he went for a pedicure and got his finger and toenails clipped.

Next he had his teeth capped and polished.

Finally he popped into Top Troll for a suit, bought some Italian leather shoes and bought some deodorant from the chemist's. It was a very different Troll who returned to Runcorn.

By the end of the day he had a new job. He was now the painter on the Runcorn Bridge.

So if you ever come to the great city of Liverpool and you drive across the Runcorn Bridge, look up.

You might just see the Troll painting it.

My Dog

My
dog
ran
like
a
mad
thing
all
the
way
home
where
he
ate my sister's
homework.
Good dog!

Robin and His Merry Men Go Large

One afternoon, in the heart of Sherwood Forest, Robin Hood, tired out after a hard afternoon outlawing, sat down with his back against a greenwood tree, pulled his feathered hat over his eyes and slipped into a deep, deep sleep.

When he came to he had the oddest feeling that something had changed. Now what could it be?

It wasn't the trees. They stood as tall as ever. It wasn't the leaves either. They turned in the wind the way they always did. It was that other sound, the strange droning in the distance. Robin stirred himself and got to his feet. He stifled a yawn with the back of his hand, made his way to the edge of the forest - which was much closer than he had remembered -...and gasped.

Suddenly his eyes were as round as saucers.

There before him was a scene from hell. Iron carriages roared along a broad, grey path. It seemed to be made of a single piece of stone. Robin raised his eyes to heaven, wondering what had happened to his greenwood home. Once more his eyes widened in amazement. There was another of those weird and wonderful iron carriages, but this one was flying.

Robin was quite dizzy with astonishment. He watched the iron carriages for a while, trying to make sense of the turn of events. After a few moments he set off along the grey, stone road towards Nottingham. He had left his Merry Men at the crossroads earlier. But the fork in the way had vanished, replaced by a huge, circular stone road. Dozens of iron carriages were whizzing round and round the circular road. Robin clapped his hands to his ears. The noise was deafening. It was madness.

Robin heard a shout.

"Hey, what's with the tights?"

Robin looked down at his clothes. What did the men in the stone carriage find so funny?

There was another shout.

"Are you going to a fancy dress party?"

Robin didn't know how to answer. He didn't know what a fancy dress party was. He stood at the edge of the road, wondering how to cross the mad, whizzing highway. He noticed a tunnel to his left. Maybe it led under the whizzing road and came out the other side. It was worth a try. He was making his way down a long slope into the tunnel when he saw a young man running towards an old lady. The young man snatched the bag she was carrying and pushed her into the wall. He then carried on into the tunnel.

Robin sprang into action. He could not stand by while the young brute treated an elderly lady so roughly. He strung his bow, pulled the arrow to his eye and loosed the shaft. It sang through the air. Robin's aim was true. A moment later the arrowhead sank into the thief's bottom. The thief howled like a stuck pig.

The old lady grabbed her bag and stared at Robin with wide, surprised eyes.

"You shot him."

"He stole from the poor," Robin said. "You are poor, aren't you?"

"Well, I'm not rich," the old lady said.

"Go on your way, good woman," Robin said. "This rogue will not trouble you again."

Unable to believe her luck, or the way her rescuer was dressed, or what he had just done, she went on her way.

"You shot me in the bum!" the thief screamed. "Are you crazy?"

"I am Robin Hood." Robin said, "I steal from the rich and give to the poor. You, my friend, are a devil in human clothing." He looked at the thief's tracksuit. "If that is indeed human clothing."

Robin was wondering what to do with the thief when he heard a noise like a thousand wolves.

"Put down the weapon!" a man barked behind him.

Robin spun round. Four men in unfamiliar, blue tunics were approaching. Their war helmets were much taller than their heads.

"Put it down!" somebody shouted from the opposite direction.

Robin turned. More men were approaching.

"Are you the Sheriff's men?" Robin asked, his hand moving to his quiver of arrows.

"Yes sure," one of the men said. "We're the Sheriff's men." He laughed and pointed to the man next to him. "And he's Maid Marian."

"He is not Maid Marian," Robin snarled. "She is fair and he is not." His eyes narrowed. "I ask again, are you the Sheriff's men?"

"If you're asking whether we are going to arrest you, the answer is yes."

The policeman had just made a bad mistake. Robin didn't understand the word police on the blue uniforms, but he knew all about the dastardly Sheriff of Nottingham and he wasn't going to let them take him prisoner. He vaulted over the railings and sprinted down the road. A motorcyclist was approaching. Robin drew his bow and pointed it at the rider's chest.

"Dismount!" he ordered.

The rider stopped and held his hands up.

"How do you make this iron horse move?" Robin demanded.

The rider tried to explain about gears and throttles.

"Enough of your gibberish, knave," Robin said. "I will work it out."

The police were racing towards him. Robin dragged the rider off the motorbike and straddled the seat. He twisted the throttle as he had seen the rider do a moment earlier. The bike reared and suddenly Robin was doing a wheelie down the road, screaming at the top of his voice. The iron horse was fighting him. While he was struggling to control the motorbike, Robin heard the noise like a thousand wolves wailing. It was the sirens of the following police cars.

Robin finally managed to fight the iron horse down to the ground. The iron horse was galloping at breakneck speed down the grey stone road. It was terrifying yet thrilling.

Robin felt the wind rushing against his face. He howled with joy. He had never had a ride like it. That's when he saw the iron man with three eyes, one red, one orange, one green. He swallowed hard. What could it be?

He decided to go faster and get past the menace. What Robin didn't know was that red meant stop. Within seconds he was hurtling through a rushing tide of speeding traffic. As he weaved in and out, screaming with terror, he clipped a car with his front wheel.

He flew…up in the air…over a van…over a fence…and landed with a splash in a stream by the side of the road. As he waded out of the stream the police screamed to a halt.

"OK, Speed King," one policeman said, "hands up."

Bewildered, bruised, battered and very bedraggled, Robin stumbled onto the bank and surrendered.

Half an hour later he was at the police station.

"I am going to charge you with grievous bodily harm," the policeman told Robin. "Do you have anything to say?"

"The harm I did was not grievous," Robin protested. "It was a good shot. I struck the knave down with a flesh wound to the right buttock. He will live."

"Are you for real?" the policeman said. "You can't go shooting people in the right buttock."

"Should I have shot him in the left one instead?" Robin asked confused. Maybe it was a local law. Only shoot a man in the left buttock.

"No," the policeman said. "You can't shoot people anywhere!"

"What, nowhere at all?"

"Nowhere."

"This is a strange land I find myself in," Robin said. "Where is it. pray?"

"What do you mean where is it?" the policeman tutted. "You're in Nottingham, my friend."

"Nottingham!" Robin cried dumbfounded. His dumb had never been so founded. "But how can that be? I do not recognize it."

The policeman shook his head and handed Robin the statement he had written. "Is this true?"

Robin read the statement. "Your English is strange but the account is true."

The policeman asked him to sign it and Robin did.

"OK," he said, "lock him up."

"But I was protecting a lady in distress," Robin cried.

"Tough," the policeman said. "Lock him up."

Robin found himself in a bare cell with a tiny window. The police had taken his bow, his sword and his hunting knife. He felt very sorry for himself. He sat thinking of his Merry Men, Mad Marian and, most of all, the unbelievable turn of events that had brought him to this place.

About the same time of day, one thousand years earlier, Robin's Merry Men were gathering round the greenwood tree where Robin had dozed off.

"This is where he vanished," Will Scarlet said.

"It's true," Friar Tuck agreed. "I saw Robin with my own eyes. I was about to hail him when he disappeared."

Little John stared at the tree. "Then this is a witching tree," he said. "It is magic."

Maid Marian stood with her hands on her hips. "If the tree carried Robin somewhere then it can take us too."

She sat where Robin had been and vanished immediately. The Merry Men stared at each other.

"Me next," said Little John.

He too disappeared. Will Scarlet and Friar Tuck followed. Within seconds all four of them had arrived in modern day England.

"It looks the same," said Marian, "but it doesn't sound the same."

They walked to the main road and stared with in disbelief, just as Robin had.

"Where are we?" Little John wondered out loud.

"I fear that this is our Sherwood," Friar Tuck said, "but many years in the future."

He was very clever. He read a lot of books. They were mostly Bibles.

They were wondering what to do when an old lady appeared, the very same old lady Robin had helped.

"Are you looking for a man in fancy dress?" she asked.

"We are looking for Robin Hood," Will Scarlet said.

"That'll be him," the old lady said. "The coppers took him to the police station."

For a moment the four friends stared then Friar Tuck made sense of her words. "Are you saying the Sheriff's men have him?"

"I suppose so," the old lady answered.

"Where have they taken him?" Maid Marian demanded.

The old lady explained.

The moon was rising by the time they found the police station. They crouched across the road and made plans. They launched their rescue about eight o'clock.

They burst through the main door and trussed up the desk sergeant with strong rope. A police constable appeared and Little John knocked him down with a blow of his staff.

"Keys," he grunted. "Where are they?"

The sergeant shook his head. "I won't tell you."

Maid Marian put a dagger to his throat. "Fair enough," the sergeant croaked. "They're over there."

The Merry Men overwhelmed the other officers on duty and locked them up. They turned the key in the lock of Robin's cell and opened the door.

"My friends!" Robin cried.

"Robin!" they shouted back.

The Merry Men were great friends, and so was the one Merry Woman. They found Robin's weapons and headed for the door. With much patting of backs and slapping of thighs they made their escape into the night.

They were making their way across the city when a man in a black suit approached them.

"Are you the band?" he asked.

"We are a merry band of outlaws," Robin answered.

"No," the man asked. "Are you the band?"

"We could be," Robin answered uncertainly.

"Look, are you the band or aren't you?" the man demanded. "I've got two hundred people waiting to be entertained and the band is late."

Just at that moment a police car appeared, siren wailing.

"We're the band," Robin said hurriedly.

The man led them through the door. Once inside the nightclub the Merry Men and the one Merry Woman stuck their fingers in their ears. They had never heard the sound of a disco before.

"I see you're already wearing your stage costumes," the man said. "On you go."

"What do we do?" Will Scarlet demanded.

"Why, perform of course."

"Perform?" Friar Tuck said. "Does he mean sing and dance?"

"I think so," Little John said. "Sing them something, Will."

Will Scarlet took the lute from his back. Luckily, he always carried it with him just in case he wanted to burst into song, which he did often. He started to play:

"My one true love

I lost today.

Hey nonny-nonny-

Nonny-nonny-no."

The crowd stared. What *was* he doing?

"A wicked rogue

stole her away.

Hey nonny-nonny-

Nonny-nonny-no."

The crowd continued to look on in stunned silence. One man booed but Little John cracked him over the head with his staff, laying him flat out on the floor. There was no more booing. The Merry Men performed several songs and Maid Marian danced with Robin. Everybody clapped politely, still wondering what they had been watching. The Merry Men passed the real band, Electric Prune, on the way out.

"We're Electric Prune," the band said.

"Good for you," Robin answered.

They snatched a few hours' sleep in a city park. It was a fine, warm night so sleeping on the benches wasn't a problem. It was for the tramps that usually slept there, of course. They weren't a bit happy. But you don't argue with men with bows, swords and staffs.

Or a woman with a dagger.

The morning sun woke them several hours later. They were all hungry but Little John was by far the hungriest. They came across a café and took their seats.

"Fancy dress party?" asked the waitress.

"You're the second person who has asked me that." Robin said, frowning.

They ordered seven full English breakfasts. There were only five of them but Little John and Friar Tuck ate two each. When they had finished Friar Tuck noticed the fridge near the counter.

"What is yonder humming box?" he asked.

"That's the fridge," the waitress said. "It's where we keep the ice cream."

"Iced cream," Tuck exclaimed. "But it is summer."

"Would you like one?" the waitress asked.

Tuck licked the ice cream and beamed with pleasure. "Delicious!" he exclaimed.

They paid with three gold coins. The waitress stared at the coins but she recognized solid gold and accepted them without question.

They were making their way down the High Street towards the site of the witching tree when they heard another of those wailing wolf sounds. An armed robbery was under way at the bank. The Merry Men and one Merry Woman leapt into action.

"Halt!" Robin cried, seeing two masked men emerging from the bank. "You did not ask my permission to undertake this robbery."

The robbers stared at each other. "We don't have to ask

permission," they said.

"Yes, you do," Maid Marian told them. "This is Robin Hood, prince of thieves."

"Yes," one of the robbers said, "and I'm Maid Marian."

"No, I'm Maid Marian," said Maid Marian.

"Why does everybody want to be Maid Marian?" Robin wondered out loud.

The robbers had had enough. They pointed their guns at Robin's band of outlaws.

"Back off," they said.

Robin didn't know anything about guns but he recognized a weapon when he saw one. He drew his bow and shot the first gun out of the robber's hands. Little John rapped the second robber's knuckles and his gun clattered on the pavement.

"Now hand over the money," Robin ordered. "It belongs to the poor."

Will Scarlet and Maid Marian tied the robbers' wrists and ankles and bound them together. They were just making off with the money when the police arrived.

"It's them again!" the first officer shouted.

"It's him again," Robin groaned.

The Merry Men and the one Merry Woman escaped into the crowded market and the police gave chase. As the outlaw band ran up the hill out of town they saw a sign.

Donkey Sanctuary.

"Mounts," Robin shouted.

Five minutes later they were riding out of the gates on five grey donkeys

"Which way?" cried Little John, hearing the police cars approaching.

Robin pointed at a blue sign. "I can see the grey stone road."

"Are you sure it's the right one?" Maid Marian asked.

"Of course it is," Robin said.

But it wasn't. They were on the M1 slip road. The donkeys and their riders joined the motorway traffic. In less than a minute they had created a huge traffic jam.

"Are you still sure it's the right road?" Maid Marian scolded.

At that very moment, Robin recognized the edge of Sherwood Forest. "There!" he shouted.

They left the motorway and set off across the fields on their donkeys. Sure enough there was the witching tree. One by one they returned home and Robin came last.

"Let's see how much we've got for the poor," Friar Tuck said.

But they were all in for a disappointment.

"This isn't real money," Little John said. "It's just blue and brown paper."

So they lit their campfire with it. They would never know that it took £100,000 to get the blaze going.

If they had they might not have been so merry.

The Teacher's Advice

Don't put jelly

in your welly.

Don't put ants

in your pants.

Don't stick asses

to your glasses.

Don't put dirt

on your shirt.

Don't put that bat

in your hat.

don't put a pie

in your eye.

Don't barf

on your scarf.

Don't put beer

in your ear.

Don't stick a rose

up your nose.

Don't get stung

on your tongue.

Don't tuck a nest

in your vest.

Don't keep a newt

in your suit.

Oh Lily, Lily, Lily

why are you so silly?

And Dwayne, yes you Dwayne,

why must you stand in the rain?

Why can't you all do

as I do?

Oh, hang on while I pour this glue

in my shoe.

Superhero for a day

Peter loved cheese, any kind of cheese.

He loved to chew Cheshire and Cheddar. He was a sucker for Stilton and Swiss Emmenthal. He was a glutton for Gruyere and Gouda. He was ravenous for Roquefort and Ricotta.

Peter really loved his cheese.

One morning, after a breakfast of Brie and crusty bread he set off for school.

He had only gone a few hundred yards when he was confronted by the oddest- looking man he had ever seen. For starters, he looked about five hundred years old. His hair was pure white and tumbled from the brim of his conical hat. His beard was equally long and white and hung over his flowing robes. Both hat and robes were deep purple and covered in silver stars and crescents.

"Are you a wizard?" Peter asked.

"I am the greatest wizard of them all?" the wizard thundered.

"Is your name Merlin," Peter asked.

"That Merlin's just a show-off," the wizard answered. "I'm Reg."

"Reg isn't a very good name for a wizard," Peter said.

"Why not?" Reg demanded.

"Well, it rhymes with veg."

"And what does Peter rhyme with?" Reg asked.

"It almost rhymes with Feta," Peter said. "That's a cheese, you know."

Reg gave Peter a long, hard look. "You're a very strange boy," he said.

"You're the one in a dress," Peter said.

"How rude!" Reg said.

"So why are you talking to me?" Peter asked.

Reg shook his head. Why indeed?

"Now listen to me, Peter," Reg said. "It is your destiny to do great things. I have been instructed by a greater power to offer you a superpower for a day. You are to use it against a great danger that is approaching."

"What danger?" Peter asked.

"The greater power didn't give me that information," Reg replied.

"But I can choose any power I want?" Peter asked.

"Anything," Reg said.

"Invisibility?"

"Yes."

"Super speed?"

"Yes."

"Flight?"

"Yes."

"Stupendous strength?"

Reg was getting impatient. "Yes, yes, yes. Anything! So what will it be?"

"Cheese," Peter said.

Reg couldn't believe his ears. "What?"

"Cheese," Peter repeated. "I want to be able to make any cheese in the world just by snapping my fingers."

"You're barmy," Reg said.

"But you've got to do what I say, don't you?" Peter said.

Reg folded his arms and sulked. "Yes."

"Cool," Peter said. "Cheese it is."

"With crackers?" Reg asked.

"Can I have crackers?" Peter asked excitedly.

"No," Reg said. "Just cheese."

"So what do we do?" Peter asked.

"Stand very still," Reg said. "One wrong move and the spell could go badly wrong. Instead of giving you the power to create cheese I could turn you into a cheese."

Peter stood very still.

"Alakazoom, alakazam," Reg said, "Alakasneeze, Alakaplease, Lord of All Powers, let's make CHEESE!"

Then he touched Peter's finger. An electric charge rang the length of Peter's arm.

"Ow," he said.

"Done," said Reg.

"So I can make any cheese I want?" Peter asked.

"Just by snapping your fingers," Reg said.

Peter snapped his fingers. Instantly half a pound of Wensleydale appeared.

"Wow!"

Reg stared at the cheese. "What good's that?" he demanded.

"What if there's a giant dragon, or a dark lord, or a serpent with a hundred heads? How are you going to stop them with a lump of cheese?"

"I'm not," Peter said, "but I can stop that."

Reg turned to see what he was pointing at...and his heart pounded.

Marching down the main street was a colossal mouse. It was at lease fifty metres high. It was kicking over cars. It was punching holes in buildings. It was trashing the town.

"Now watch," Peter said.

He marched forwards and produced a huge chunk of Red Leicester. The mouse sniffed hungrily and followed him. Peter threw the mouse the cheese and the mouse gobbled it down. Peter ran a hundred yards down the road and produced a huge chunk of Gorgonzola. The mouse followed. Peter threw the mouse the cheese and the mouse gobbled it down.

This went on for about ten minutes then the mouse stopped. It gave the most horrible squeak. It gave a huge burp. Then it shrank to the size of an ordinary mouse and scampered away never to be seen again.

"Amazing!" Reg said. "How did you know what to do?"

"Easy," Peter said. "I know my cheese."

"It only took you half an hour to save the world," Reg said, impressed. "What are you going to do with the rest of the day?"

Peter magicked an enormous chunk of Double Gloucester and smiled.

"Guess."

Pin

Our
Teacher
Got
So
Mad
His
Head
Exploded.
You
Could
Hear
A
Pin
Drop.

Shrunk!

Millie was a curious child. She had always been that way. Her first word was *why*.

Why is the sky blue?

Why do babies cry?

Why does it always rain on Sundays?

Why, why, why?

She took everything apart to see how it worked.

How does this thing move that thing?

How does a clockwork toy keep going?

How does a magnet stick to iron?

How, how, how?

The day Mr Invento moved in next door Millie became even more curious.

What were those banging noises in the night?

What make the colourful flashes she could see in his windows?

What was he up to?

What, what, what?

One Saturday morning her curiosity got the better of her. She was bursting to find our what Mr Invento was up to. She crept up his garden path and stood on her tiptoes so she could see inside. Her eyes widened. There, in the middle of the living room, stood a silver machine. It was all gauges and knobs and levers. There were dozens of coloured lights that were flashing on and off.

What could it be?

Millie caught sight of Mr Invento. He was tinkering with something that looked like a long blue fuse. Mr Invento was an odd-looking man. His hair was frizzy and bright orange. He was still in his pyjamas and slippers. They all had teddy bear designs. His eyes were hidden behind wrap around, mirrored sunglasses. Mr Invento finished what he was doing with the fuse and slipped it into the silver machine. His tabby cat rubbed itself against his legs.

"Let's see if this works, Mr Tibbles," he said.

It started to whirr and hum then it shuddered to a halt. Mr Invento put his hands on his hips and shook his head.

"Another failure."

He seemed to think for a moment then stamped out of sight. Mr Tibbles followed.

This was Millie's chance. She crept inside and edged over to the silver machine. She started to examine it.

Where did he put that valve?

Where does the power come from?

Where's the on button?

Where, where, where?

More importantly, what did it do?

Millie pulled a lever here. She pushed a button there. Nothing happened. Finally she lost her temper with the stupid thing and gave it a kick. The machine rumbled to life. The lights glowed and flashed. The engine thudded and grumbled. Millie peered into the huge golden light bulb at the front. Suddenly there was a blinding glare.

Millie blinked for a few moments, unable to see properly. When the black spots cleared from her eyes she looked around and swallowed hard. The chairs were as tall as a house. The table was as big as a mountain. Everything was so enormous.

"Which means," Millie said out loud, "I must have shrunk!"

It was true. She was no taller than a pencil.

She rushed to the silver machine. It towered above her. How do I get up there and reverse it, she wondered. She was still trying to find a way up when she heard a low growl behind her. She turned slowly…and screamed. It was Mr Invento's tabby cat, Tibbles. At least it had been a tabby cat when she was normal-sized. Now it looked like a sabre tooth tiger the size of an elephant.

"Nice Mr Tibbles," she said.

But Mr Tibbles was being anything but nice. He crouched low. The hair rose on the back of his neck. He bared his teeth.

"Bad cat!" Millie said, wagging her finger.

Mr Tibbles hissed.

"Oh no," Millie groaned, "now I've upset him."

Mr Tibbles started to move forward, one huge paw at a time.

"Go away," Millie cried. "Boo! Shoo!"

Mr Tibbles crouched low.

"Bad cat!" Millie shouted. "Bad, bad cat!"

Mr Tibbles prepared to attack.

"No!" Mille screamed, putting her hands over her face.

But nothing happened.

When she removed her hands Mr Tibbles had gone. Millie looked left. She looked right. Then she looked up and saw Mr Tibbles in Mr Invento's arms. Mr Invento had picked him up just in time.

"Mr Invento," Millie shouted. "Hey, Mr Invento."

But Mr Invento hadn't even seen her. Mr Tibbles was clawing at Mr Invento's pyjamas, trying to get down.

"What's this?" Mr Invento said. "The machine has started up all by itself. Now how did it do that?"

Mr Tibbles started mewing.

"Are you trying to tell me something, Mr Tibbles?" Mr Invento asked.

Millie looked around for somewhere to hide. She spotted Mr Invento's floor length curtains. She scrambled up as quickly as she could and jumped onto Mr Invento's desk. She armed herself with a pair of scissors and waited for Mr Tibbles to come looking for her.

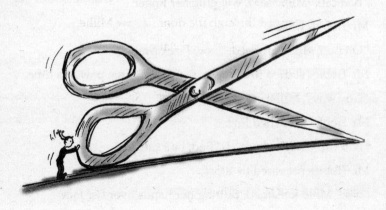

Mr Invento continued to tinker with his machine. Mr Tibbles continued to watch Mollie. Mollie waited with a pair of scissors she could barely even lift. The afternoon wore on and the sun sank lower in the sky. Mr Invento finally gave up on his machine and left the room. Now it was just Mollie and Mr Tibbles. The room darkened and Mr Tibbles' emerald eyes glittered through the gloom. Mollie swallowed hard.

If I get out of here, she promised herself, I will never be nosy again.

It got darker and darker. Mum will be worried, Mollie thought. Dad will be angry. Then Mr Tibbles made his move. He started to pad forward, a menacing growl rumbling in his throat. Mollie gripped the scissors. Mr Tibbles hopped onto the table. Mollie struggled to lift the scissors. Mr Tibbles sprang. Mollie launched the scissors at him with all her might. Seeing the scissors coming at him, Mr Tibbles miaowed in panic and leapt from the table. The scissors flew past him and bounced off the silver machine. There was a blinding glare and the room was normal sized again. Mr Invento walked into the room. He had heard the noise. The moment he stepped through the door he saw Millie.

"There's a girl on my desk!" he exclaimed.

Millie gave a nervous wave. "Hi."

Mr Invento saw her staring at the silver machine. "Ah, I see you've noticed the Shrinkovator. Is that what brought you into my living room?"

Mollie nodded.

"Would you like to see how it works?"

"No thank you," Millie said. "I should go home. It's getting dark."

"Of course," Mr Invento said. He picked up the cat that was rubbing himself against his legs and purring. "Have you met Mr Tibbles?"

Millie saw the hungry way Mr Tibbles was looking at her.

"Yes, we've met."

"Would you like to stroke him?"

Millie shook her head. "I'd rather not."

She ran all the way home and closed the door behind her. She didn't see the blinding glare in Mr Invento's living room. She didn't hear the frightened cry of:

"Mr Tibbles!"

What's more, she never saw Mr Invento again.

Kenning

Face-twister,

Stair-stamper,

Computer-hogger,

Long -scowler,

Fridge prowler,

Spot-squeezer,

Sibling-teaser,

Sometime sulker,

Guess who?

Your teenage brother.

My teacher's an alien

We always knew there was something odd about Mr Kozmik. Maybe it was the way he seemed to glide into class. Maybe it was that funny little red light that appeared in his eyes from time to time. Maybe it was the way he made high-pitched, bleeping sounds every now and then.

Then there was that time at the zoo. Whenever he stopped to look at the animals they started to act strangely. The elephants trumpeted and backed away. The hyenas stopped laughing and cowered in a corner. The monkeys fled to the top of the trees. The big, brown bears turned their backs and covered their ears. Even the lions slunk away and hid. There was something unusual about Mr Kozmik.

Things came to a head one afternoon. We were doing maths. Mr Kozmik was showing off, doing the 147 times table...backwards. Suddenly he checked his watch and smiled.

"Time for a bit of science," he said.

Even as he spoke a pair of antennae rose from the back of his head.

"How did you do that?" Danny Wilson asked.

"It's easy when you come from the planet Vingo 5," Mr Kozmik answered.

"What do you mean?" Danny asked.

Mr Kozmik winked. "Watch."

The blackboard flipped over, replaced by a chart of the solar system. The floor started to tremble.

"What's happening?" Danny asked.

Shutters slammed down over the classroom windows.

"I don't like this," Jennie Harris said.

"Me either," Riz Khan said.

Together they bolted for the door but a shutter blocked that off too.

"Let us out!" they wailed.

"Sorry," Mr Kozmik said. "No can do. Now excuse me while I make myself comfortable."

He reached round the back of his neck and unzipped his skin. Out came something green and slobbery with one big eye in its forehead and half a dozen squirming tentacles. All the kids screamed and ran to the other side of the room.

"Don't be scared," Mr Kozmik said. "I don't bite…very often."

He thought that was funny. He had a bad sense of humour, that Mr Kozmik.

Our adventure had only just begun. There was a loud roar and the classroom broke free from the rest of the school. It must have left an almighty hole.

"The classroom's a spaceship," Danny cried.

"Well duh," Riz said. "The rest of us worked that out ages ago."

The spaceship rose steadily into the air.

"Shouldn't we have seatbelts?" Jennie asked.

"If it was a primitive Earth ship you would," Mr Kozmik said. "But this is a Vingo Spacesprinter XL19. You won't float round the room. Your ears won't pop. Your nose won't bleed. We solved all those problems years ago."

He was still speaking when everybody's hair stood up on end.

"Oh, that's one thing we haven't solved. Or the flatulence."

"What's flatulence?" Danny asked.

We found out a moment later when there was a noise like thirty gunshots

"Ewww!" everybody cried.

Mr Kozmik just gave a big, slobbery laugh. He was enjoying himself.

"Where are we going?" I asked.

"Would you like to see?" Mr Kozmik said.

He opened one of the shutters and there was planet Earth far below us. It was the size of a grapefruit, then a plum, then it was gone.

"We're on our way to Vingo 5," Mr Kozmik explained.

"Is this some kind of school trip?" Jennie asked.

"Yes," Mr Kozmik said, winking with his one big eye. "It's a school trip."

Somehow I didn't believe him. What was he hiding?

The journey to Vingo 5 took four hours. Finally we saw a huge purple planet looming in the window. We plunged through boiling scarlet clouds and set down in the middle of an enormous glass and steel city that stretched as far as the eye could see. Spacecraft zipped this way and that on highways in the sky. Mr Kozmik opened the door.

"Take a look around," he said.

Something in his voice told me we weren't going to like what we saw. For a few moments we spread out around the spaceship staring at the two suns, the racing spacecraft, the buildings that stretched way up into the scarlet clouds.

"Are we going to look round?" Riz asked.

"Oh, you won't be seeing much of Vingo 5," Mr Kozmik said.

No sooner were the words out of his mouth than collars snapped round our necks. From everywhere more slobbery octopus aliens like Mr Kozmik appeared and started dragging my friends into spacecraft.

"Where are you taking us?" Danny wailed.

"Where do you think?' Mr Kozmik said. "You're all going to be exhibits in our Space Zoo."

"But we're not animals!" Danny protested.

"Are you sure about that?" Mr Kozmik scowled. "I've seen you eating in the dining room!"

An hour later all thirty of us were sitting in an enclosure just like the ones at our zoo back home. There were grassy banks and boulders. Tyres hung from trees. There was a pool. Here and there food lay rotting on the ground.

"I don't like it here," Danny moaned.

"Oh, stop whining, Danny," I told him.

Visitors to the zoo started to arrive. All manner of weird and wonderful alien creatures stared at us. Some tried to make us perform for them. Others threw food. Danny ran round picking it up.

We all wanted to know what he was doing.

"I'm hungry," he explained.

He was about to tuck in to his feast when…it moved. The thing that looked like an apple jumped out of his hand and ran off over the rocks. The object that looked like a bun tried to bite him. The stuff that looked like spaghetti started to wriggle and squirm like a mass of worms. Danny dropped the whole lot and screamed in disgust.

"It's alive!"

That's when Mr Kozmik appeared in the crowd. "Of course it's alive," he said. "All food on Vingo 5 is alive. That's what makes eating it so interesting."

"You're not just weird," Riz shouted. "You're sick!"

That made the whole crowd roar with laughter. Moments later everybody was pelting us with live food. But none of it was edible.

The things that looked like bananas leaked stinky, yellow slime.

The things that looked like pork pies smelled of sweaty socks.

The things that looked like chocolate bars oozed maggots.

Everything was disgusting.

"Maybe we could try eating the grass," Jennie suggested.

Then the grass blew a raspberry at her. We couldn't even do that.

"But we've got to eat something," Danny groaned.

But we didn't, not that day. Not the next. Everybody was getting really thin.

On the second evening, when the Zoo had closed for the day, Jennie called everybody over.

"Hey, look at this," she said.

In the next enclosure there was a creature called a Hopdepottamus. It was the size of a rhino or, well, a hippopotamus. But there was a big difference. It was yellow and it could hop about thirty metres in the air.

"Can you understand us?" Jennie asked.

The Hopdepottamus nodded.

"If you can jump," she said, "why don't you just jump over the wall and run away?"

"I would," the Hopdepottamus answered, "but I have no sense of direction. No Hopdepottamus knows his north from his south, or his east from his west. That's why we are so easy to keep."

"What if you got us out and we showed you which way to go?" Jennie said.

The Hopdepottamus thought for a few moments then he called the rest of the herd over. They talked for quite a long time, pausing now and then to look at us over their shoulders. Finally, the Hopdepottamus leader came over to us.

"We'll do it," he said. "But you've got to promise to take us home to our planet."

"Done," Jennie said.

"But how do we fly the spaceship?" I asked.

Jennie shrugged. "I have no idea."

She really didn't but it was better than starving to death in the Space Zoo.

The Hopdepottamuses started bouncing up and down in excitement.

"Sh," Jennie said. "You'll alert the keepers."

One by one the Hopdepottamuses hopped over the wall into our enclosure. Each of them could fit half a dozen kids on their backs. Soon we were hopping towards the spaceship landing pad where we had arrived. The guard was asleep so we crept quietly aboard.

"How do we fly it?" Riz wondered, pushing all the buttons.

He pushed a red one and the spaceship filled with choking smoke.

"Oops, wrong one."

"What about this one?" Jennie asked.

She pushed the black button and we rocketed into the sky. Soon we were on our way to Hopdepottamum 10, the Hopdepottamuses' home planet. We dropped them off, thanked them and set course for planet Earth. It was really easy. All you had to do was use the black button as a mouse and point it towards the star chart. You chose your constellation. Click. You chose your star. Click. Your chose your planet. Click.

Simple.

Easy as hopping on a Hopdepottamus's back.

We landed on the school field. It wasn't long before hundreds of parents, teachers and policemen surrounded us. For days we had to ask millions of questions. The trouble was, nobody believed the answers.

Our new teacher was called Miss Lewis. She was very nice. She didn't have antennae or tentacles or anything like that. One day in the summer term she told us she was planning a school trip. "What about the zoo?' she asked.

She looked really surprised when we all replied with one voice: "No-o-o-o-o!"

Epitaph

Here lies Humpty Dumpty.
People say he was cracked
But that might be a bad yolk.

If it looks like a dragon and sounds like a dragon....

What was that?

Billy sat up in bed, knuckling the sleep from his eyes. He listened. There it was again. Something was tapping on his window. Maybe it was the branch of that old apple tree in the garden. Billy shook his head. No, the tree was too far away. The tapping started once more. Rain? No, it was too regular, too loud. It was as if somebody was trying to wake him up.

"Well, you've managed it," Billy grumbled, padding across the carpet in his pyjamas and bare feet.

He drew the curtains…and gasped. There before him floated a most remarkable creature.

It flapped its wings like a dragon.

It had scales like a dragon.

It whipped its tail back and forth like a dragon.

It breathed fire and smoke like a dragon.

"If you look like a dragon," Billy stammered, "and sound like a dragon….then you must be a dragon."

"That's right," the dragon said. "I'm a dragon." He chuckled. "Hi, my name's Donny."

"What kind of name is that for a dragon?" Billy asked.

Donny frowned. "Actually, it's a very good name for a dragon. What's wrong with it?"

"Nothing, I suppose," Billy said.

"What's your name?" Donny asked.

"Billy," Billy told him.

"There you go," Donny said. "You're Billy the boy and I'm Donny the dragon. It makes perfect sense."

"Maybe it does," Billy said, "but why were you tapping on my window."

"It's like this," Donny said. "We dragons have been getting a very bad press. We're supposed to burn maidens to a crisp and eat knights in shining armour. That's silly. I don't like overcooked food and I certainly don't like canned food."

Billy looked horrified.

"Joking," Donny said, "just joking. You've nothing to fear from me. I'm a vegetarian dragon."

"Really?" Billy asked.

"Really," Donny answered. "You don't catch me eating maidens, knights or little boys."

"That's OK then," Billy said.

"Anyway," Donny said, "the Dragon Council decided to send some of us out to educate you humans. We are to give selected children a ride to Dragonia- that's Dragon Land to you- and show them we're friendly."

"So you want me to go with you?" Billy asked.

"Yes please," Donny said. "I've got references."

He handed Billy his references. Billy read them.

"See," Donny said, "I am a very safe dragon. I am a very friendly dragon."

So Billy accepted Donny's invitation. He opened the window, climbed onto the window sill and scrambled up Donny's back.

"Hold tight," Donny said.

Billy put his arms found Donny's neck.

"Up, up and away!" roared Donny.

Instantly, they shot into the night sky like a bullet from a gun. He was thrown back along Donny's back and just managed to hold on. The wind rushed in Billy's face making him blink. When he was at last able to open his eyes he stared at the world far below. House lights blinked. Car headlights sprayed onto motorways. Airliners swept past them.

"We're flying!" Billy cried.

"We certainly are," Donny said. "It's much quicker than walking, and more fun."

They flew on through the night. The world rushed by beneath them. They glided over mountains high and valleys deep, snow-capped peaks and gleaming lakes, rolling plains and dark, dark forests. They looped round the Eiffel Tower and sat for a moment at the top of the Empire State Building. They soared over the summit of Mount Everest and dipped low over the Pacific Ocean. All in all, they did the world tour.

"Are you enjoying the ride?" Donny asked.

"I'm loving it," Billy laughed.

Soon they left the towns and cities behind and raced across desert wastes and empty steppes.

"Not long now," Donny said.

Billy was getting excited at the thought of Dragonia.

"There it is now," Donny announced.

Billy peered through the rushing clouds and there it was, set on a plateau atop a huge, dark mountain, Dragonia, the land of the dragons. Billy had never seen so many dragons. In fact, until this evening, he had never seen a single dragon. Now they were everywhere.

There were dragons in suits and dragons playing flutes.

There were dragons on skates and dragons lifting weights.

There were dragons playing tennis and dragons called Dennis.

There were dragons skiing and dragons hee-heeing.

There were dragons pogoing and dragons ho-hoing.

There were dragons of every shape and size, of every colour and every hue.

"Cool!" Billy said.

"It is cool," Donny agreed. "Would you like an ice cream?"

"Yes please," Billy.

When the ice cream came the cone was bigger than Billy and the flake was as tall as a tree. Donny had to hold it while Billy licked the ice cream and nibbled off bits of chocolate.

Donny took Billy to meet his mum and dad. They were teachers at Dragon County High School. Donny's Dad said Billy was really very nice for a human and Donny's Mum said he was a proper little gentleman, much better than those awful dragon slayers who gave humans such a bad name.

Finally Billy did an interview on Dragon TV. He told the interviewer that he thought dragons were very nice and he would be saying so when he got home. The dragons in the audience applauded loudly.

Finally it was time to go home. Billy fell asleep on the way back and Donny tucked him up very gently in his own comfy bed. Then he said goodbye to the sleeping boy and flew all the way home to Dragonia.

Billy never forgot his night flight to Dragonia. From that moment on, whenever anybody had anything bad to say about dragons he was sure to stick up for them. Of course that wasn't very often. Not many people have seen a dragon.

Well, have you?

In a naughty kid's pocket

In a naughty kid's pocket

you might find:

chewing gum (at least three days old),

a burnt match,

a chewed bus ticket,

a felt tip pen,

a toenail,

the teacher's patience,

a lock of blond hair,

a mouse - dead obviously,

my pocket money.

That's what you'd find

in my brother's pocket.

Bear-faced cheek

The smell of porridge wafted through number five, Grizzly Drive waking Daddy Bear. He propped himself up on one elbow and groaned. He had had one pint too many of his favourite Bear's Bitter down at the Bruin Arms. He had a banging head, bloodshot eyes and a mouth like the inside of a black bear's cave. He felt *terrible*.

He brushed his teeth slowly to save his aching head. It didn't do any good. Every sound made his head bang: the toothbrush, the running water even the spitting.

He stumbled downstairs, wincing as he put each paw down. Maybe a bit of breakfast would do the trick.

"Good morning, dear," said Mummy Bear. "Did you have a good night out with the boys?"

"Too good," grunted Daddy Bear. "My head hurts."

"A nice bowl of porridge will do you the world of good," Mummy Bear told him. "Tuck in."

Daddy Bear took one swallow and rushed to the sink with his mouth on fire. He stuck his head under the tap and swallowed mouthful after mouthful of cold water.

"What are you trying to do to me?" he groaned. "That porridge is red hot."

"You should have tested it first," Mummy Bear told him. "You don't just stick it in your mouth, you silly old bear."

"That does it," Daddy Bear said. "We're going to go for a walk. By the time we get back the porridge will have cooled down a little."

"Go for a walk?" Mummy Bear said. "But that's just silly. Put some milk on it. Put it in the fridge. Fan it with your hat."

But Daddy Bear insisted his way was best. Soon he was walking round the local park with Mummy Bear and their son, little Darren Bear. Nobody noticed that Daddy Bear had forgotten to lock the door.

While the three Bears were enjoying their walk a local scalawag by the name of Miss Goldie Locks was passing. She had bright orange hair, a leather jacket and skirt, spangly blue tights and bovver boots. She was chewing gum and she had R&B playing on her IPod. When she noticed that the front door was open. She decided to take advantage of Daddy Bear's forgetfulness.

Goldie crept up to the open door. "Anyone in?" she called.

There was no answer.

"Is anybody there?"

There was still no answer so Goldie went in. She saw three bowls of porridge on the table. She sat right down and started eating the first bowl. Like Daddy Bear she stuck the first mouthful straight in her mouth. Also like Daddy Bear she thought it was too hot. She rushed to the sink and stuck her head under the coldwater tap.

"That porridge is too hot," she said.

She tried Mummy Bear's bowl.

"Yeuch," she said, "that porridge is too cold."

Then she tried Darren's bowl. "Mm," she said, "that's just right."

So she ate every mouthful, leaving the bowl empty.

Having finished her breakfast, she decided to have a sit down.

She tried Daddy Bear's chair. The cane stuck in her bottom.

"Far too uncomfortable," Goldie said.

She tried Mummy Bear's chair. It nearly swallowed her up.

"Far too soft," Goldie said.

Finally she tried Darren's chair.

"Now that," she said, "is what I call a chair. It's just right."

At least it was until it broke under her. After all that eating and sitting in chairs and breaking them she was quite exhausted so she went upstairs to find somewhere to have a nap. She tried Daddy Bear's room. It had four guitars, a drum kit and posters of The Beatles and Elvis Presley on the walls.

"Far too rock 'n roll," she said. "So yesterday's music."

She tried Mummy Bear's room. It had a soft bed and lots of chintz.

"Far too girly," she said.

Finally, she tried little Darren Bear's room. There was a gorgeous bed with a Marvel Comic duvet and posters of all her comic book characters.

"Now this," she said happily, "is just right."

And it was. She drifted off to sleep, snoring contentedly.

About the same time the three bears came round the corner after their walk.

"Can I have my breakfast now?" Darren asked grumpily.

Mummy Bear smiled. "Of course you....Uh oh."

"What's the matter?" Darren asked.

Mummy Bear pointed. The front door was wide open. She glared at Daddy Bear.

"I told you to lock the door," she said.

"Oops," Daddy Bear said.

"I'll give you oops if we've got mean, nasty burglars in the house," Mummy Bear told him. "Right, go and see if we've got intruders."

"You don't really think we've got burglars, do you?" Daddy Bear asked.

"There's only one way to find out," Mummy Bear told him.

So Daddy Bear walked up to the door armed with the yard brush.

"Is anybody there?" he called inside.

There was the noise of Goldie snoring. Zzzzzzzzz.

"Oo-er," Daddy Bear said, his fur standing up on end, "it sounds like we've got burglars."

"That's your fault, you big lump," Mummy Bear said. "You'd better chase them out."

"But they might not want to go," Daddy Bear said, trembling.

"So make them," Mummy Bear said. "Now!"

Daddy Bear tiptoed into the hall clutching his yard brush. Shaking like a leaf, he called up the stairs. "Can you hear me, Mr Burglar? There are ten of us and we've all got great big, fierce dogs with us."

But Goldie was fast asleep and she snored loudly. Daddy Bear looked over his shoulder, lip quivering.

"He won't go."

"So make him," Mummy Bear said. "Stop being a cowardly custard. You're a bear, aren't you? Act like one."

Daddy Bear crept up the stairs and pulled a balaclava from the landing cupboard.

He put it on.

"Do I look fierce?" he whispered.

"You look silly," said Darren, trying hard not to giggle.

Daddy Bear took a deep breath and peered into his room.

There was nobody there.

He eased open Mummy Bear's door and looked inside.

There was nobody there either.

"The burglar's in your room, Darren," he whispered. By now Daddy Bear was shaking so much he looked like a furry jelly.

"Go on," Mummy Bear hissed. "Get him!"

"Can't you do it?" Daddy Bear asked.

"No way," Mummy Bear answered. "Who left the door open?"

So Daddy Bear puffed himself up as big as he could and burst through the door.

"Raaaaarghh!" he roared.

"Aaaaaarghh!" Goldie screamed.

"You're a girl!"

"You're a bear!"

They stood looking at each other for a moment then Daddy bear kind of smiled. Goldie kind of smiled back.

"Did you get the burglar?" Mummy Bear asked.

"She's not a burglar," Daddy Bear said. "She's a little girl."

Mum planted her paws on her hips. "She's a very naughty girl. She ate Darren's porridge. She broke his chair. She slept in his bed. What kind of behaviour is that?"

"What if I put it all right?" Goldie asked.

"Then we'll forgive you," Mummy Bear said.

"Even you?" she asked Darren.

"Even me," Darren said.

So Goldie made a new bowl of porridge with extra honey. She mended Darren's chair. She even made Darren's bed and tidied his room.

And she did it all just right.

The tale of the cute little ant

Once upon a time there was a rude, little ant,
And such a boastful, little ant.
"I'm the best, little ant,
and the cleverest, little ant,
and I am so much better than you,"
                                        said he.

But he was such a cute, little ant
And such a handsome, little ant.
People looked at him and smiled.
"You're the cutest, little ant
and the handsomest, little ant,
that I can't be angry with you,"
                                        said they.

One day the rude, little ant,
That boastful, little ant
Saw a man standing in his way.
 "You're an ugly, big man
and such a stupid, fat man,
you're standing in my way,"
                                        said he.

But the man in his way,
Who wasn't fat or ugly by the way
But was deaf so they say
Without an instant's delay
Stood on that ant
Right away
And left him squashed and dead.
                              Aw!

Fast-foot Frankie

This is the story of an eight-year-old girl who won the Grand National, an FA Cup Semi Final and the World Tap Dancing Championship all in the same day. Incredible? You'd think so, wouldn't you?

But Francesca 'Frankie' Ford was no ordinary little girl. Her parents and teachers called her a Tomboy, though she hated that nickname. I'm not a boy, she would yell, I'm a GIRL! What's wrong with a girl liking wrestling, football, rugby, keeping beetles, rolling in mud and punching little boys on the nose? She climbed every tree, jumped over every stream and dared every dare.

She was a tearaway, a corker, a mischief.

One day Frankie went on a school trip. She loved the park. She could run around, play football, row boats, pull faces at animals, climb trees and tease boys. But she hated the museum.

It was so bo-o-o-o-oring.

Frankie's teacher Mr Bootle saw how bored Frankie was. He pointed out a pair of shoes in a glass case.

"Come and look at this, Frankie," he said.

Frankie looked at the glass case and turned up her nose. "What's so special about a pair of smelly, old shoes?" she asked.

"These aren't just any pair of smelly, old shoes," Mr Bootle said. "They used to belong to Marvellous Mickey Mitchell."

"Who's he?"

"Who *was* he?' Mr Bootle said. "Marvellous Mickey Mitchell died years ago. He was the last Englishman to win the World Tap Dancing Championship. That was fifty years ago."

"Boring," Frankie said.

"It's not boring," Mr Bootle said. "Do you know why the shoes are on display? Fifty years after Marvellous Mickey Mitchell won the World Tap Dancing Championship in Paris. This year's Championship is being held right here in Liverpool, his home town." He lowered his voice. "There's a rumour that Mickey's ghostly feet still haunt these shoes."

Finally Mr Bootle had Frankie's attention. Did he just say they were haunted?

Mr Bootle went to separate the Dooley twins. They were fighting again. Frankie gazed at the shoes. Haunted, eh? That sounded so cool. Imagine if they were. What would it be like to wear haunted shoes?

I've got to try them on, she told herself. She was only going to borrow them for a few minutes. Once she had had a go, she would put them back. She looked left. She looked right. Nobody was looking. Very carefully, she opened the case and took the shoes out. They didn't look so special. She unlaced her own shoes and put them in the glass case in place of Marvellous Mickey Mitchell's tap shoes.

She slipped them on, and waited…and waited…and waited.

"They're not special at all," she grumbled.

She was about to take them off when she felt something. There

104

was a tingle in her toes then a sizzling sensation along the soles of her feet. She wanted to dance. In fact, she *had* to dance.

Mr Bootle called the children over. "It's time to get the coach back to school," he said.

Frankie couldn't keep her feet still. Tip tap went the shoes.

"Frankie," Mr Bootle said. "Keep still please."

She tried to tell him she had to do something.

'No time," Mr Bootle said, glancing at his watch. "We've got to go."

Tip tap went the shoes.

"Frankie," Mr Bootle said. "I'm not telling you again."

"But."

"No buts," Mr Bootle said. "Now everybody follow me."

Frankie didn't know what to do but the shoes did. They danced all the way onto the coach. Frankie couldn't stop them. Back at school Frankie tried to tell Mr Bootle what had happened but the shoes just danced away with her feet in them. She danced all the way home. She was still dancing when she got home. What was she going to do? She finally managed to get them off. She fell asleep and dreamed of dancing feet.

Next morning she woke up. She didn't wear the shoes. She was scared of what they might do. She put on her slippers and went down to breakfast. It was Saturday. There was no school. Frankie had the whole day to herself.

"It's a big day today," Dad said. "There's an FA Cup semi final between Clamborough United and Flickerby Rovers, there's the greatest horse race in the world, the Grand National and there's the World Tap Dancing Championship. I bet you don't know why they're special."

"Yes I do," Frankie said. "Marvellous Mickey Mitchell won it for England fifty years ago today and he was from Liverpool."

"Very good," Dad said. "I always knew that was a good school." Frankie didn't think any school could be good. But why think about school? She had a whole weekend to do anything she wanted. She ran upstairs and got dressed. Without thinking, she put on the shoes she had borrowed from the museum...and that's when the fun started.

Immediately she started dancing furiously. She danced downstairs, startling the cat. She danced outside, scaring the dog. She danced down the street, stopping the traffic. She danced so fast her feet became a blur. As she danced past the supermarket she saw Mr Bootle. He was out shopping with his wife. He didn't see her either. There was a kind of blur and a rush of wind and a voice that screamed:

"Mr Booooooooooootle!"

By now Frankie was dancing so fast she was leaving a trail of sparks and flame down the road. She danced up to the T-junction and onto the dual carriageway. She recognized the road. She was dancing towards the football stadium. She danced through the turnstiles and into the stadium. Soon she was dancing across the pitch. She saw the scoreboard. It read Clamborough United 1 Flickerby Rovers 1. The game was in the 92nd minute. Extra time was looming.

The shoes had a life of their own. Frankie danced into the centre circle and dispossessed Dumbaldo, United's new Brazilian midfielder. She skipped past the tackles of Ivan Thuggic, the centre half, and Lou Roll, the right back and slotted the ball into the net through the flailing arms of Italian goalkeeper Eco Friendly. The crowd were stunned. Frankie had been dancing so fast they hadn't seen her.

Nobody had disposed Dumbaldo.

Nobody had skipped past those tackles.

Nobody had scored.

Nobody had celebrated.

But somehow United had won 2-1.

As 48,000 fans, 22 players and three officials wondered what had just happened, Frankie was already dancing down the road to Aintree where the Grand National, the greatest horse race in the world, had just started. Frankie danced through the gates and onto the racecourse. She danced over Becher's Brook and passed Look Lively, the 100-1 outsider. She danced over the Canal Turn and passed Funky Chicken, the favourite. She cleared the Chair and closed on the second horse, Darned Tooting. She took the Water Jump neck and neck with Ee Ba Gum, the leader. The shoes tapped even faster and she passed the finishing line. She, or rather the shoes, had won the Grand National.

Even then, the shoes weren't finished. Frankie danced along the River Mersey to the Echo Arena where the World Tap Dancing Championship was taking place. For the first time in an hour Frankie danced to a stop.

"Are you a late entrant?" the man at the desk asked.

The shoes tapped frantically.

"I think so," Frankie said. "Yes."

She tapped through the semi finals and danced to victory in the final. When the judges gave her the trophy she knew what to say in her acceptance speech.

"I owe everything to Marvellous Mickey Mitchell," she said.

The crowd clapped. The shoes tapped. After the competition Frankie gave the shoes back.

But the trophy she kept.